S0-ARY-211

by Michael Hardcastle

Illustrated by Tony O'Donnell

Librarian Reviewer
Allyson A.W. Lyga
Library Media/Graphic Novel Consultant
Fulbright Memorial Fund Scholar, author

Reading Consultant
Elizabeth Stedem
Educator/Consultant, Colorado Springs, CO
M.A. in Elementary Education, University of Denver, CO

STONE ARCH BOOKS
Minneapolis   San Diego

First published in the United States in 2007
by Stone Arch Books,
151 Good Counsel Drive, P.O. Box 669,
Mankato, Minnesota 56002.
www.stonearchbooks.com

Originally published in Great Britain in 2000
by A & C Black Publishers Ltd,
38 Soho Square, London, W1D 3HB.

Text copyright © 2000 Michael Hardcastle
Illustrations copyright © 2000 Tony O'Donnell

All rights reserved. No part of this publication may be reproduced
in whole or in part, or stored in a retrieval system, or transmitted in
any form or by any means, electronic, mechanical, photocopying,
recording, or otherwise, without written permission of the publisher.

Library of Congress Cataloging-in-Publication Data
Hardcastle, Michael.
    [Sam's Dream]
    Sam's Goal / by Michael Hardcastle; illustrated by Tony O'Donnell.
    p. cm. — (Graphic Trax)
    Originally published with the title: Sam's Dream 2000.
    ISBN-13: 978-1-59889-088-4 (hardcover)
    ISBN-10: 1-59889-088-3 (hardcover)
    ISBN-13: 978-1-59889-234-5 (paperback)
    ISBN-10: 1-59889-234-7 (paperback)
    1. Graphic novels. I. O'Donnell, Tony, 1957–. II. Title. III. Series.
PN6727.H375S26 2007
741.5'9—dc22   2006006071

Summary: When England's top goal-scorer invites Sam to his next soccer game, he can't
believe it. The problem is, neither do Sam's friends.

Art Director: Heather Kindseth
Colorist: Mary Bode
Graphic Designer: Kay Fraser
Production Artist: Keegan Gilbert

1 2 3 4 5 6 11 10 09 08 07 06

Printed in the United States of America.

TABLE OF CONTENTS

Cast of Characters

SAM

ANTONY

MOM

ALEX

DAD

Chapter One

Sam saw the ball coming right to him. It was a kick from the right and Sam was sure he could score a great goal.

Sam darted forward. He kicked the ball powerfully, but then watched it sail over the bar.

Sam wailed, squeezing his eyes shut and banging his fists down on his bare knees.

Sam's had been thinking about Alex Ackton only a split second earlier. Ackton scored goals for the All Stars, the greatest team in the world.

But still, you got away from the player guarding you, so that was good. And you took a shot. That was good, too.

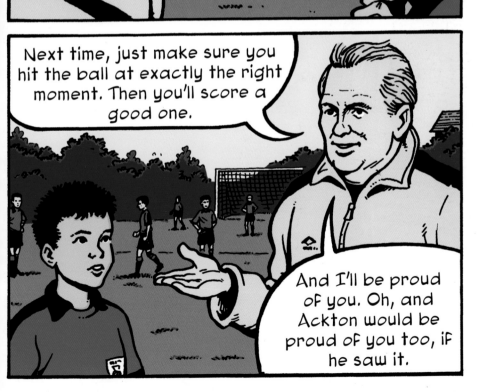

Next time, just make sure you hit the ball at exactly the right moment. Then you'll score a good one.

And I'll be proud of you. Oh, and Ackton would be proud of you too, if he saw it.

When it was time for a break, Sam sat down behind the goal. He was still wondering how he had missed that shot.

He wanted to be the top scorer for his team, the Alden Aces. He wanted everyone to see that he was a great player who would play for the All Stars some day. Just like his hero.

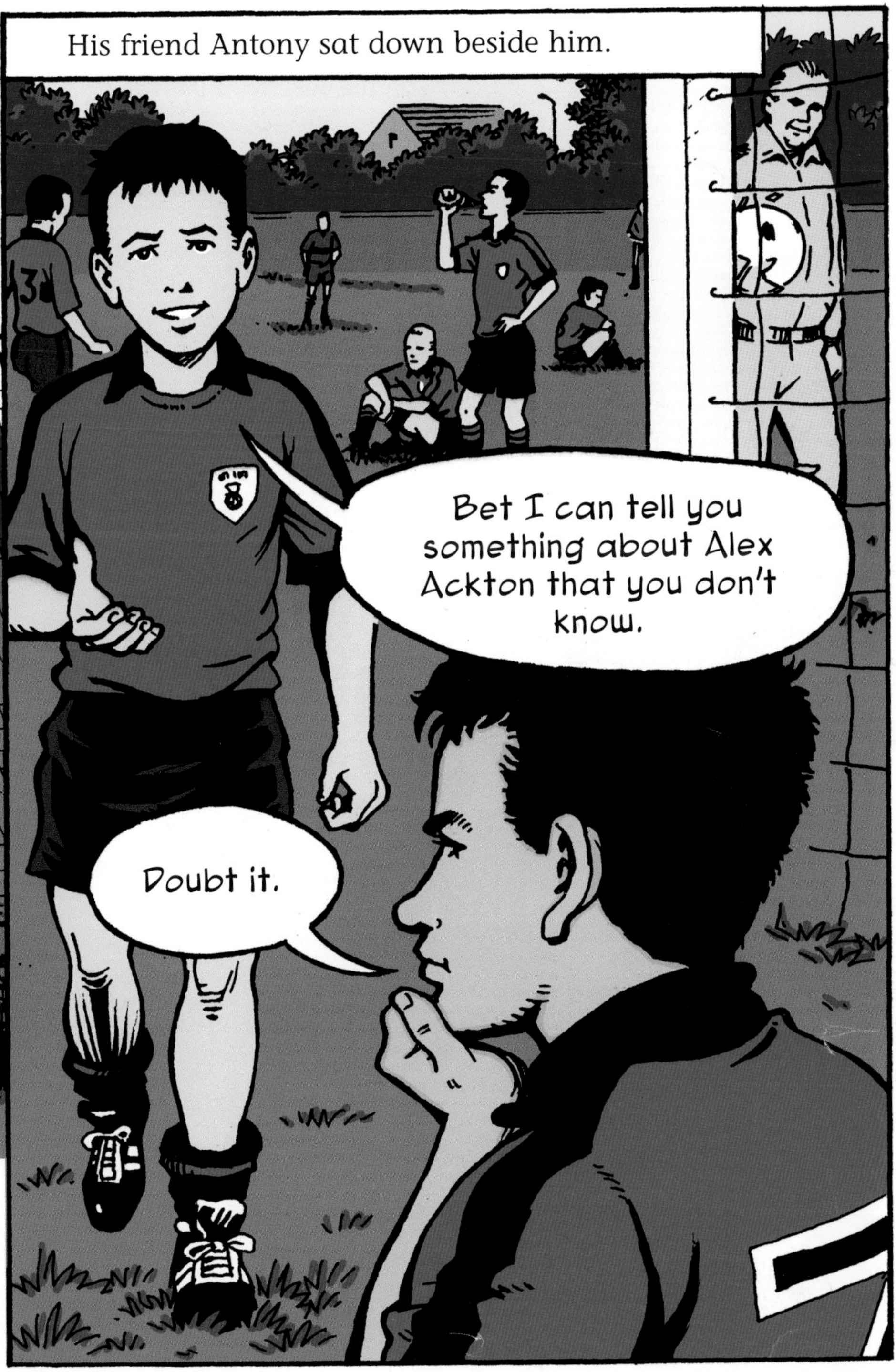
His friend Antony sat down beside him.
Bet I can tell you something about Alex Ackton that you don't know.
Doubt it.

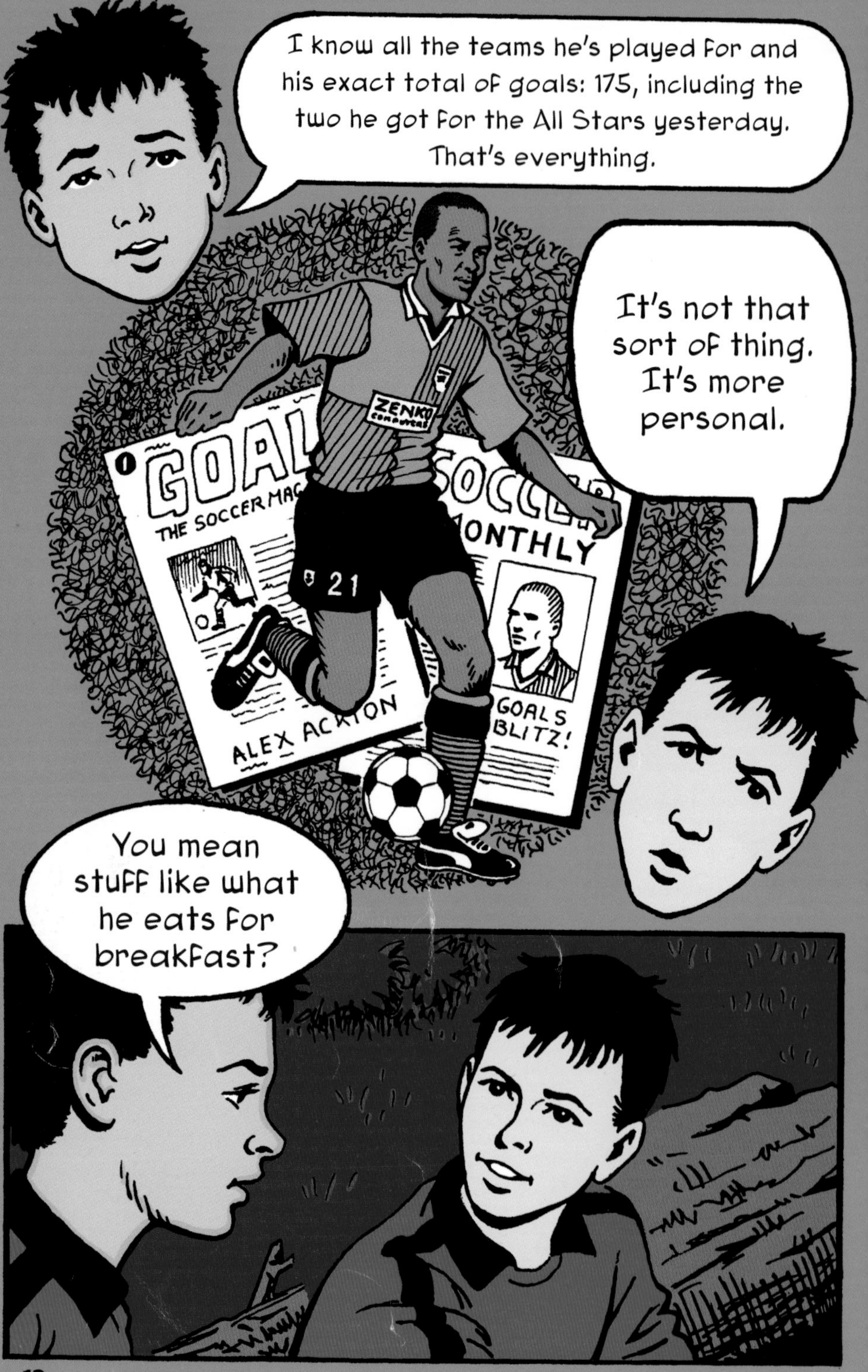
I know all the teams he's played for and his exact total of goals: 175, including the two he got for the All Stars yesterday. That's everything.
It's not that sort of thing. It's more personal.
You mean stuff like what he eats for breakfast?
GOAL THE SOCCER MAG
ALEX ACKTON
SOCCER MONTHLY
GOALS BLITZ!
ZENKO
21

Sam had to think. Everyone knew Ackton was married and had a baby son named Thomas. There had been a lot in the newspapers about the star player's joy at becoming a dad.

Sam admitted defeat, which was unusual for him. His mind was still on that missed goal.

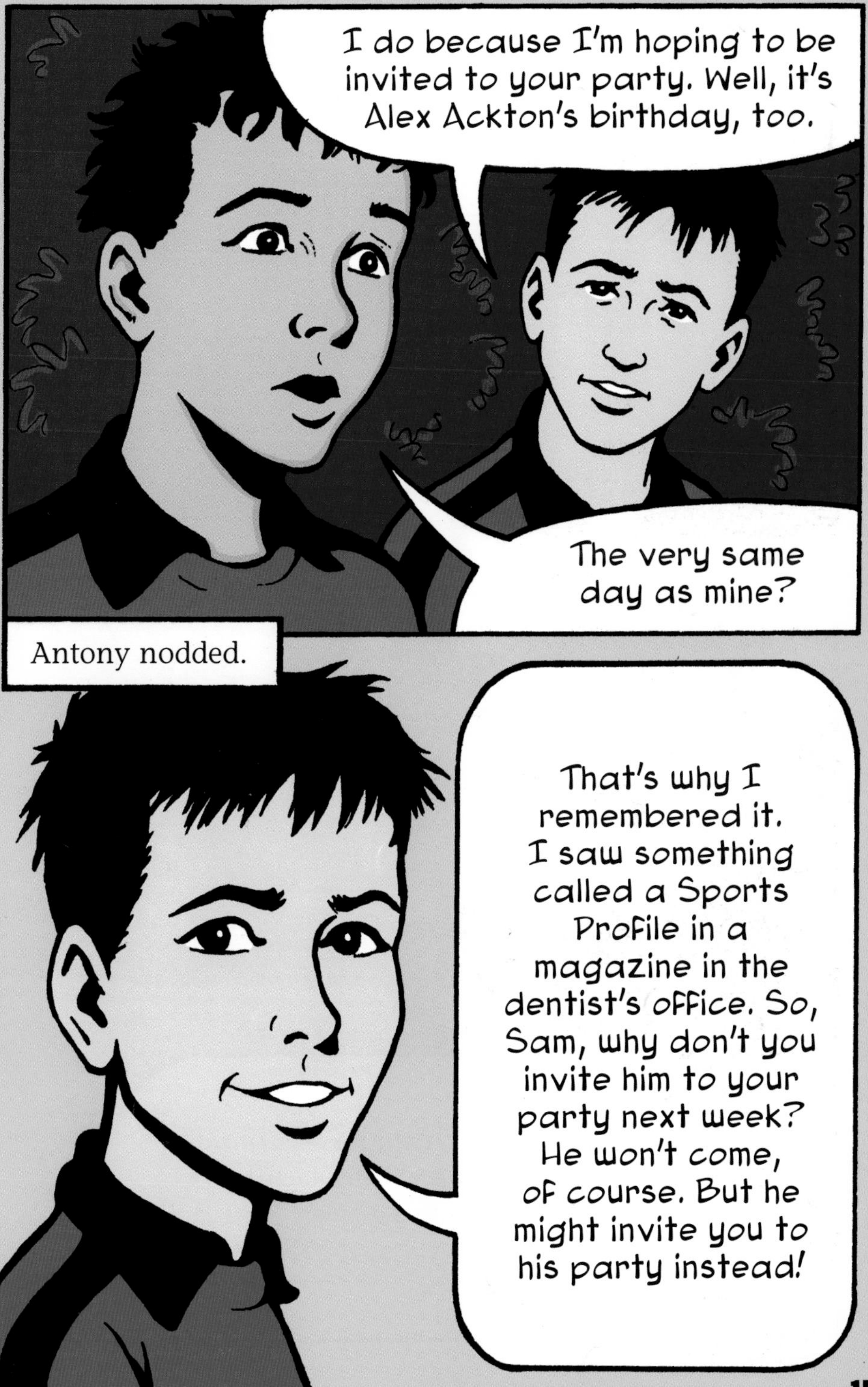
I do because I'm hoping to be invited to your party. Well, it's Alex Ackton's birthday, too.
The very same day as mine?
Antony nodded.
That's why I remembered it. I saw something called a Sports Profile in a magazine in the dentist's office. So, Sam, why don't you invite him to your party next week? He won't come, of course. But he might invite you to his party instead!

Sam was stunned. To think that his hero actually shared his birthday! He jumped to his feet and gave his friend a big bear hug.

Terrific idea, Antony! Thanks for thinking of it. You'll definitely be at my party. If Alex comes, I'll get him to give you a special autograph or something.

When practice started again, Sam found it hard to think of anything else but his hero.

Luckily, the coach was upset with Edward, who said he didn't want to be a defender. So when Sam made a mistake, the coach didn't say a word about it.

Chapter Two

When Sam got home, he asked his mom and dad right away.

Can I invite Alex Ackton to my birthday?

Please?

Who? The famous soccer player?

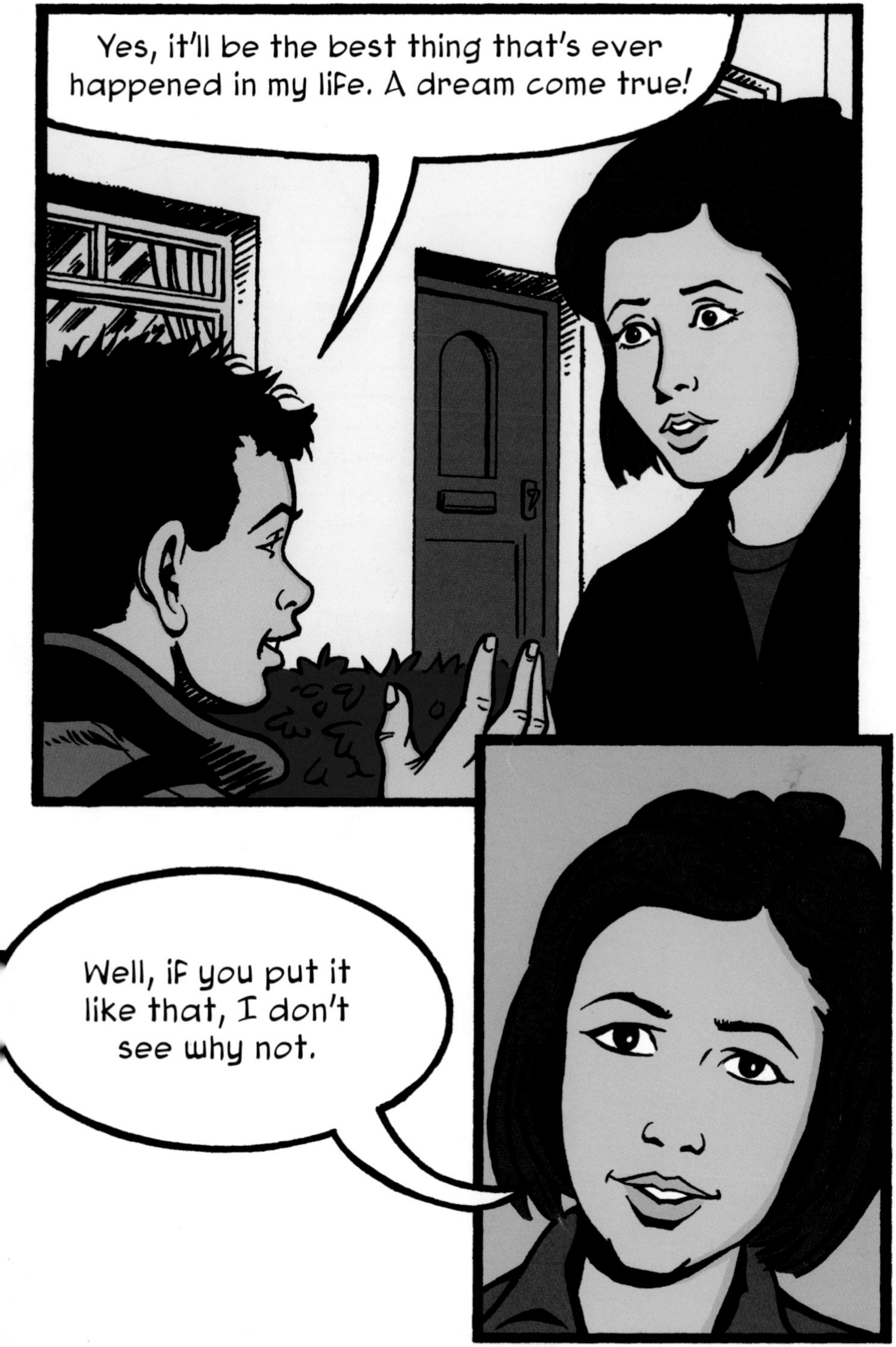
Yes, it'll be the best thing that's ever happened in my life. A dream come true!
Well, if you put it like that, I don't see why not.

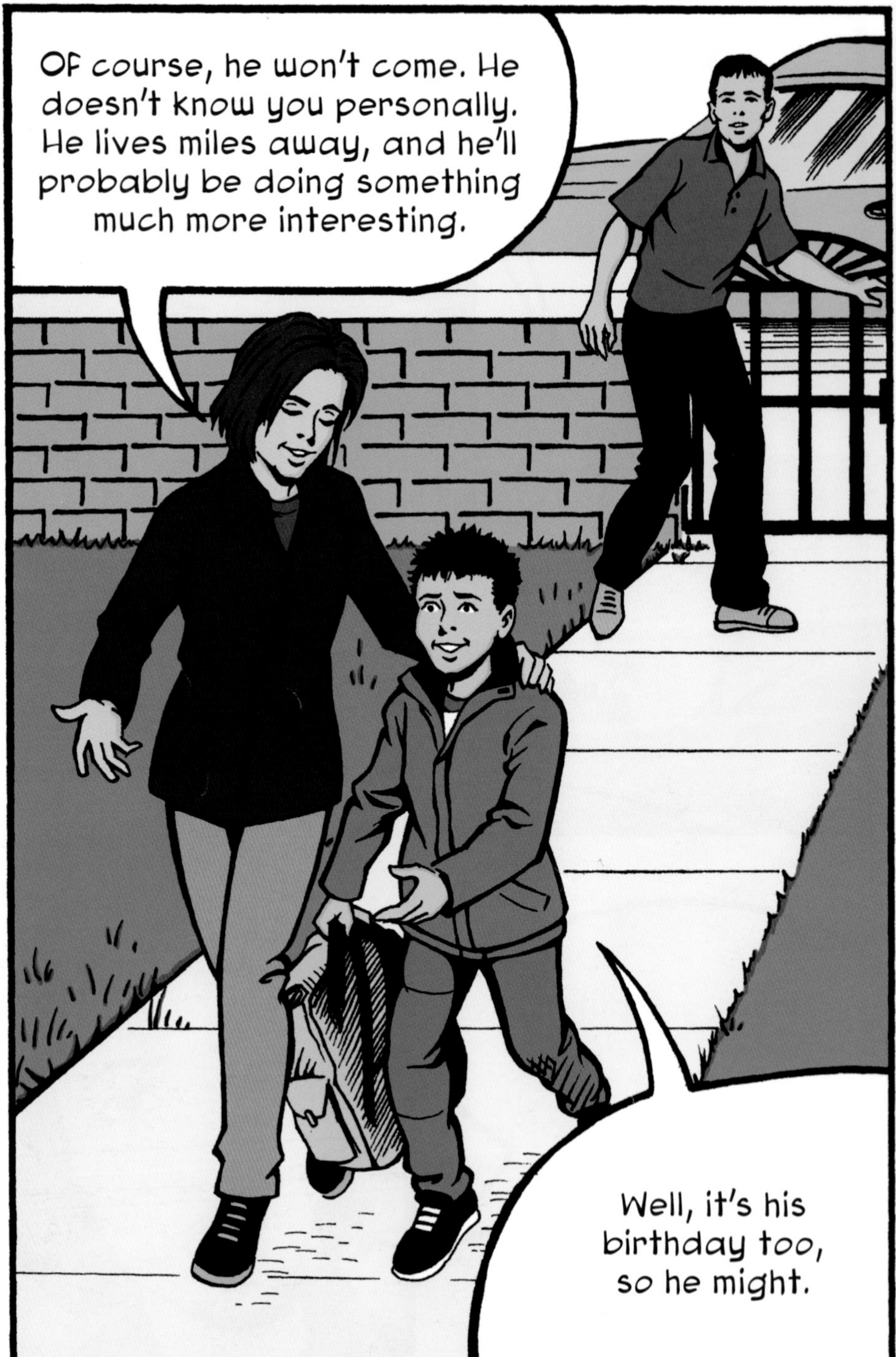
Of course, he won't come. He doesn't know you personally. He lives miles away, and he'll probably be doing something much more interesting.
Well, it's his birthday too, so he might.

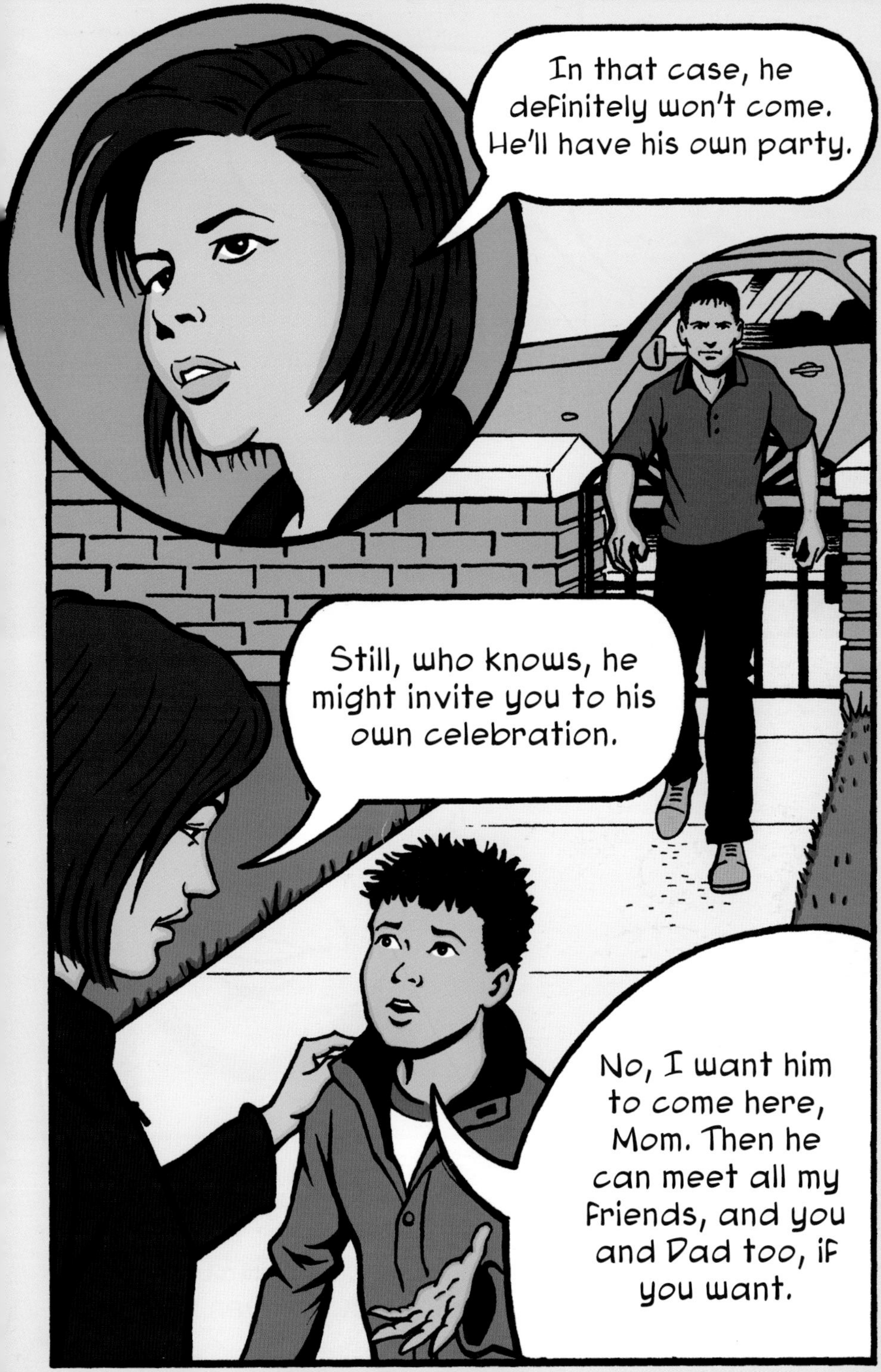
In that case, he definitely won't come. He'll have his own party.
Still, who knows, he might invite you to his own celebration.
No, I want him to come here, Mom. Then he can meet all my friends, and you and Dad too, if you want.

You write the letter, Sam. I'll find the team's address. That's where we'll have to send it because Ackton's home address is a secret, except to the people he has given it to.

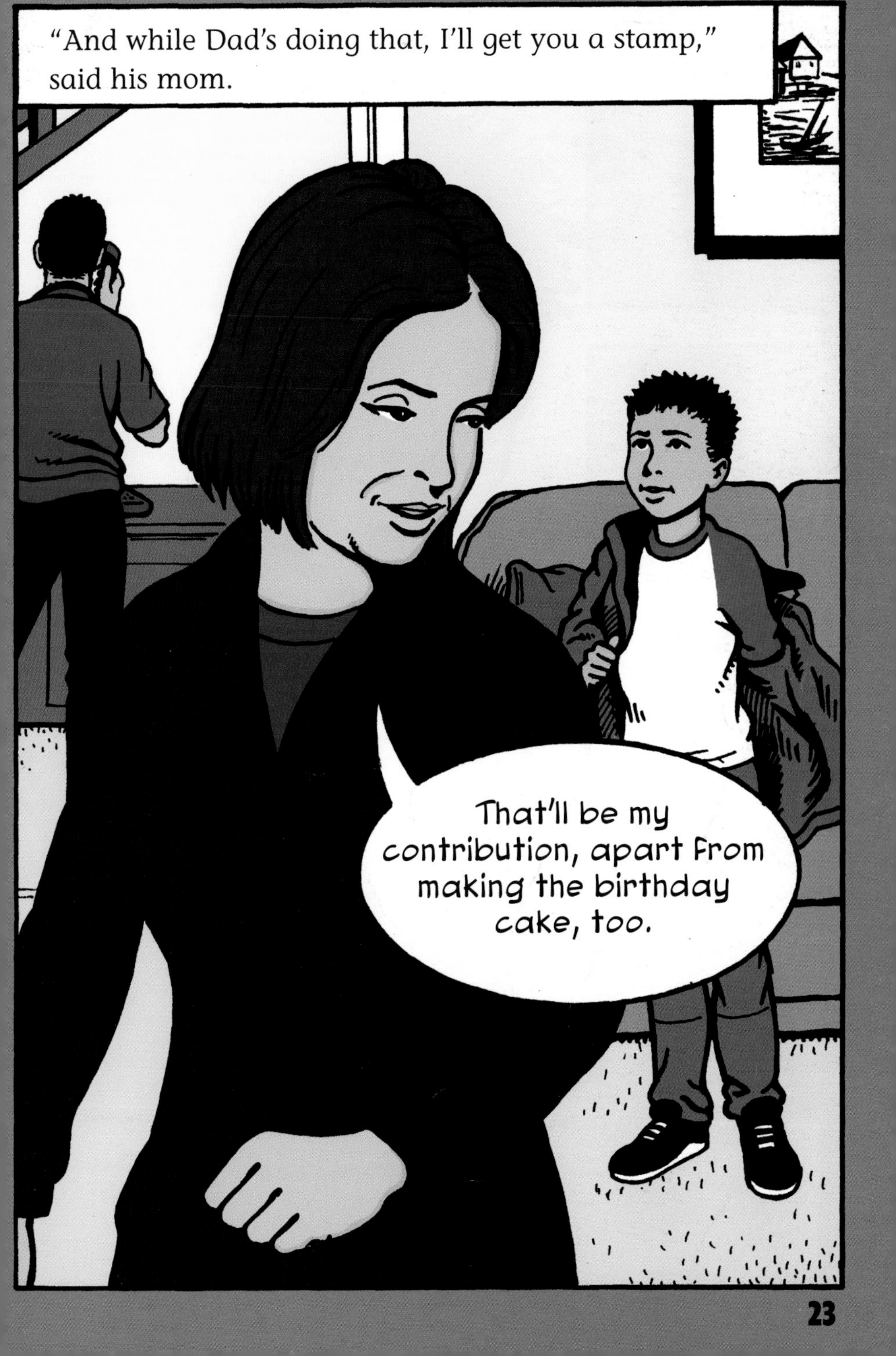
"And while Dad's doing that, I'll get you a stamp," said his mom.
That'll be my contribution, apart from making the birthday cake, too.

After a few minutes, Sam came up with the final
version of his letter to the world's best player.

Dear Mr. Ackton,

Please would you come to my birthday party? My birthday and your birthday are on the same day, October 14th. I'm a big fan of yours and I'd like to meet you. My mom makes great cakes. So please say you'll come. We'll have all sorts of other food because my dad is a great cook, too.

Your #1 fan,
Sam Stevens.
P.S. I'm a goal-scorer, too. (but not as good as you)

His dad read it.

It's a good letter, Sam. I'm sure you'll get a reply. Would you like me to send it for you?

Sam's dad worked at the post office, but Sam wanted to make sure the letter was sent right away. So he thanked his dad, but told him he'd like to put it in the mailbox at the end of the street himself.

Chapter Three

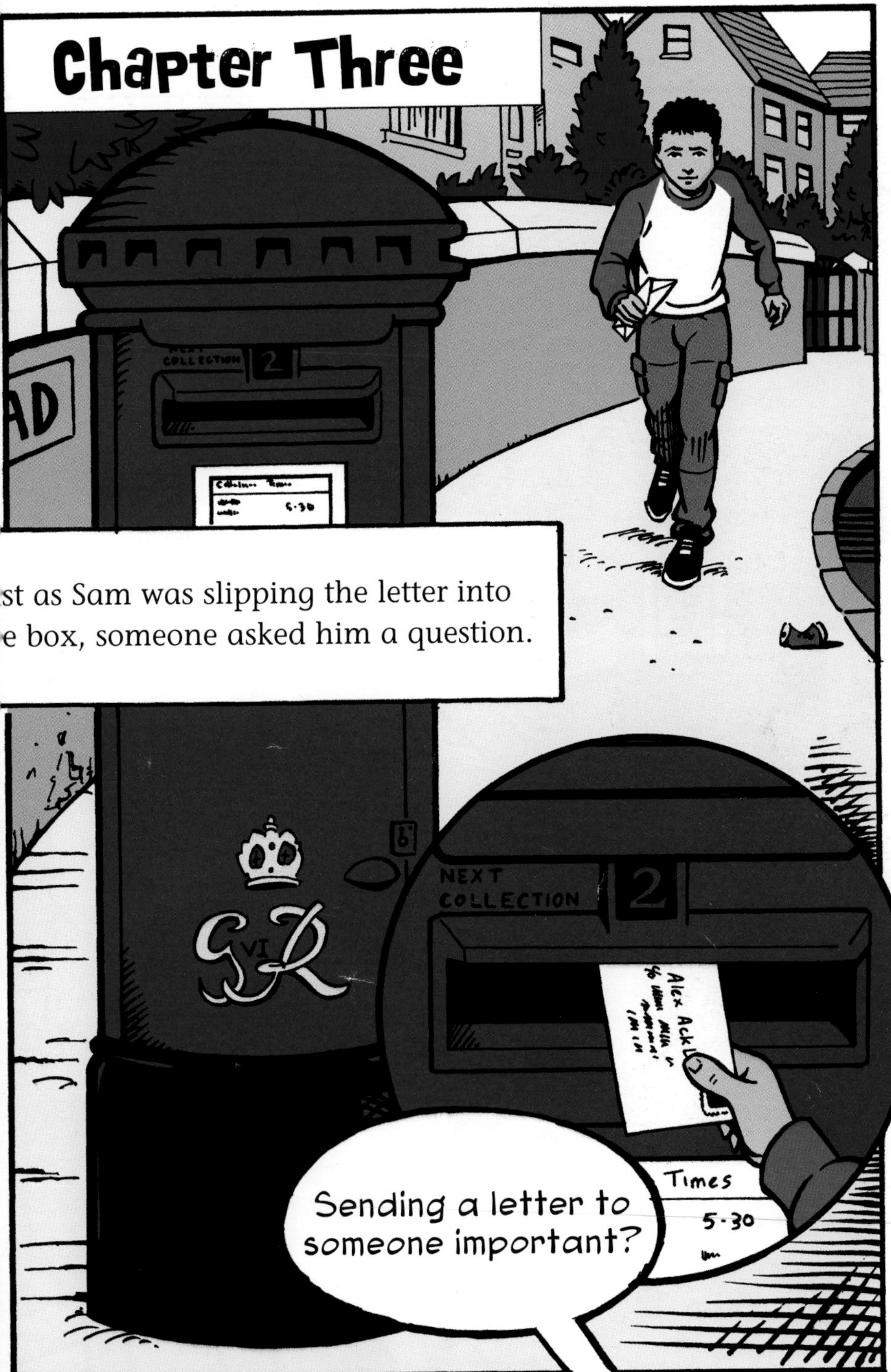
st as Sam was slipping the letter into
e box, someone asked him a question.
NEXT COLLECTION
2
Times
5-30
Sending a letter to someone important?

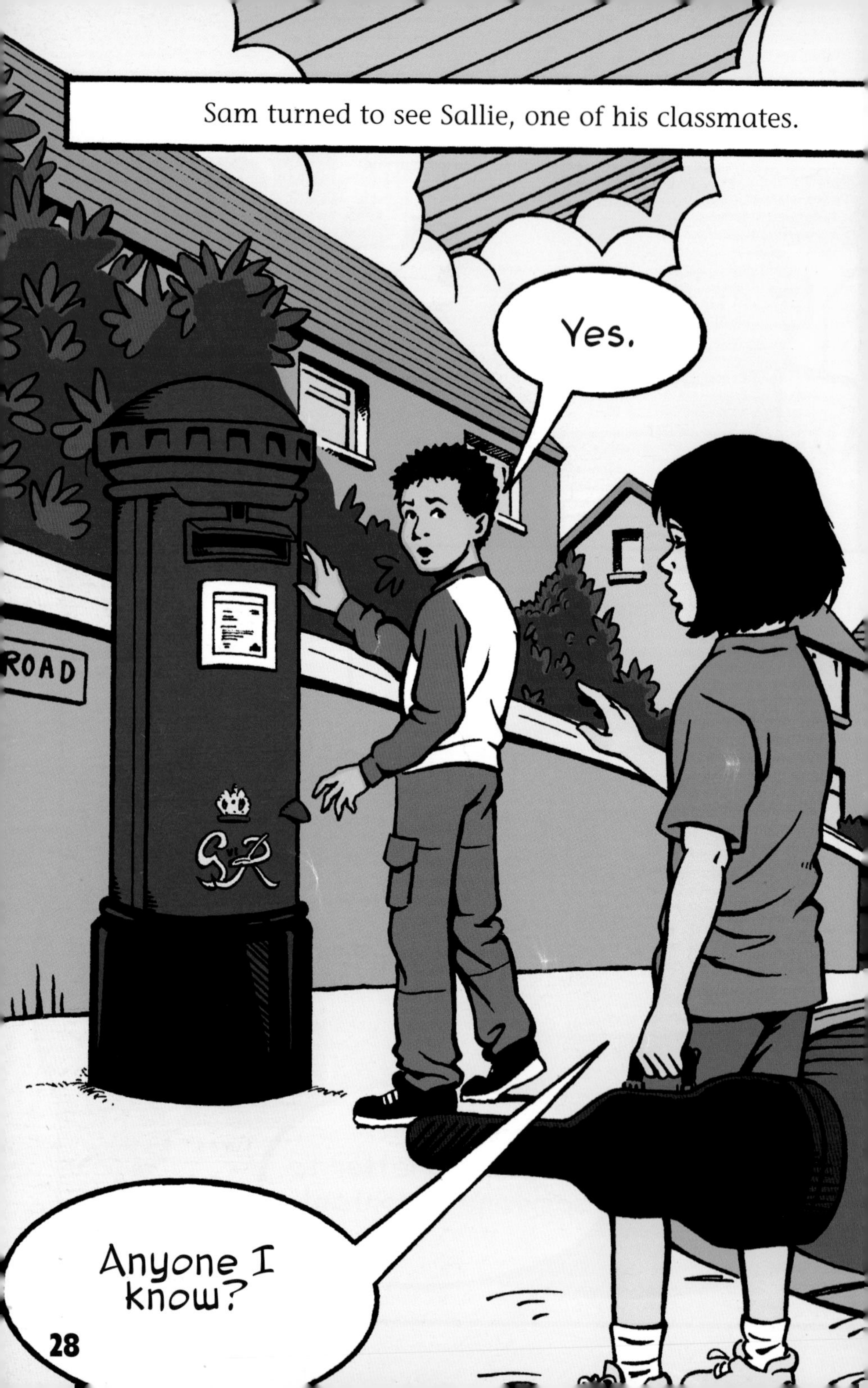
Sam turned to see Sallie, one of his classmates.
Yes.
ROAD
Anyone I know?

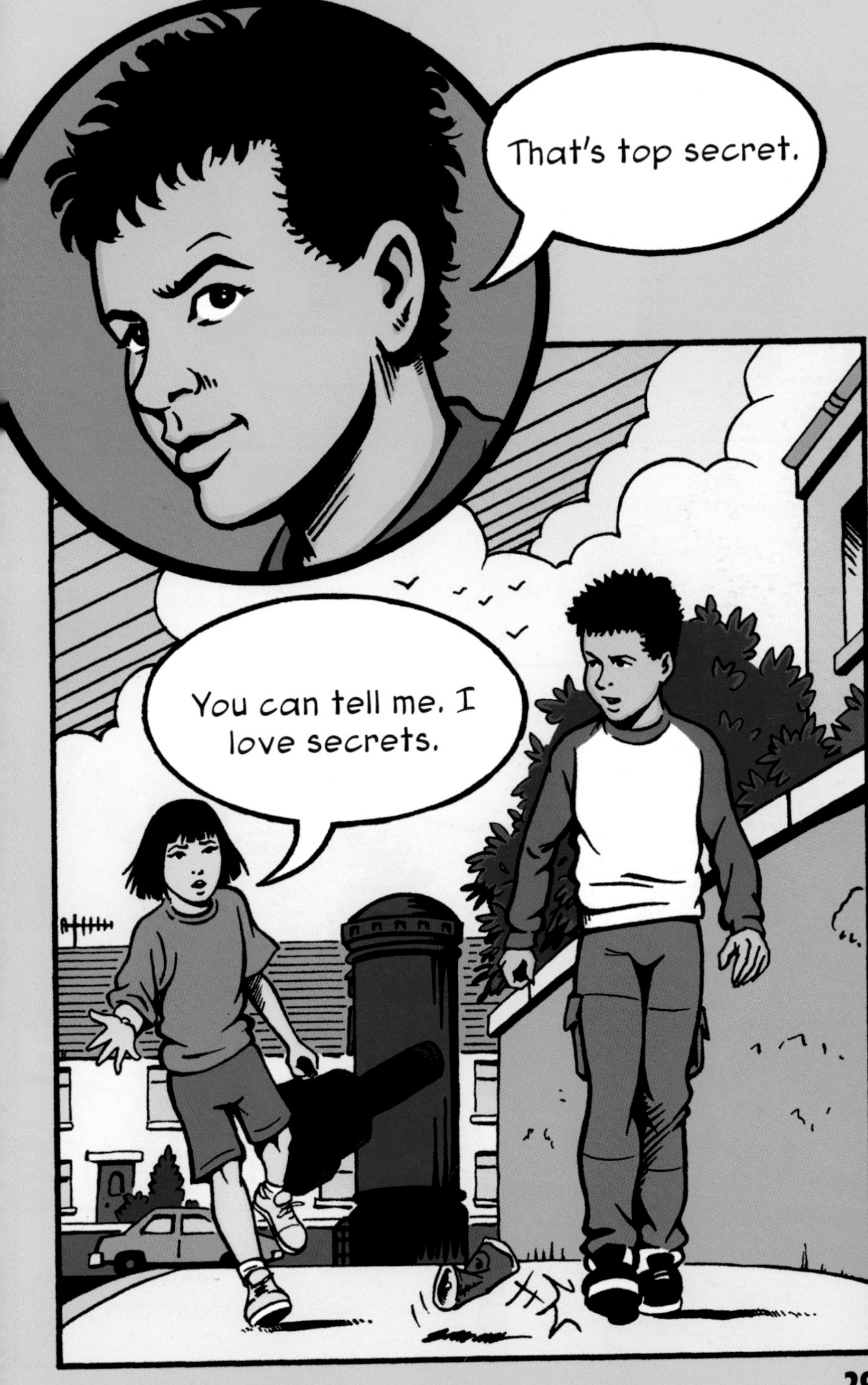
That's top secret.
You can tell me. I love secrets.

He saw how disappointed she was. He liked her because sometimes she lent him books and comics. "You can play soccer with me and Antony tomorrow, if you like," he said.

"Suit yourself," said Sam, setting off for home. He wondered how long it would take his hero to reply to the birthday invitation. The letter would probably arrive the day after tomorrow.

Chapter Four

No letter arrived on any day. Within a week, however, there was a phone call. Mom answered the call and her eyebrows shot up.

"Hello, Sam, I'm pleased to speak to you," said the voice. "This is Alex Ackton. Thank you very much for your letter and the invitation to your party."

Sam gasped when he could finally speak. It was almost impossible to believe his hero had called him.

"Thing is, Sam, I'll be out with my family on our birthday. It's a family thing, so I can't really invite you," Alex went on. "But the All Stars are playing the Lightning, your local team, in your town in November. So come to that game as my guest, with your mom and dad, too. What do you think?"

That's cool, Alex. I mean, Mr. Ackton.

"Oh, call me Alex. Everyone else does! Well, that's good, Sam. Got to go now but I'll be in touch again when I've organized the tickets and everything. Okay?"

"Oh, one more thing. Don't forget to keep scoring those goals of yours," said Sam. And then there was silence at the other end of the line.

Sam's parents seemed as stunned as Sam was when he told them, practically word for word, what the great scorer had said to him.

"Well, it worked, that letter of yours," his dad said. "I told you it was a good one, didn't I?"

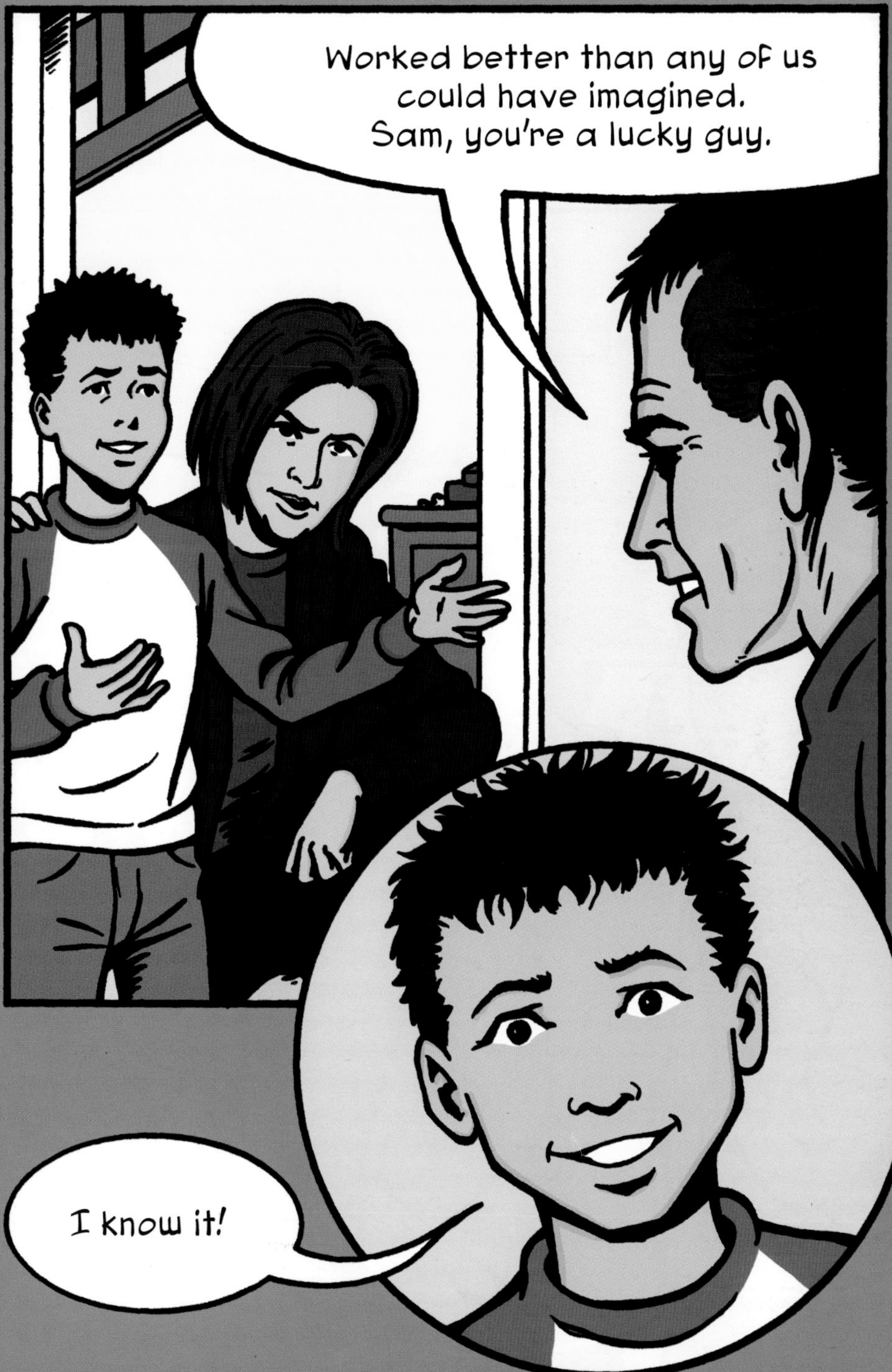
Worked better than any of us could have imagined. Sam, you're a lucky guy.
I know it!

His teammates didn't think so. But that was because they didn't believe Sam's story of a phone call from the famous player. They were sure he was making it up.

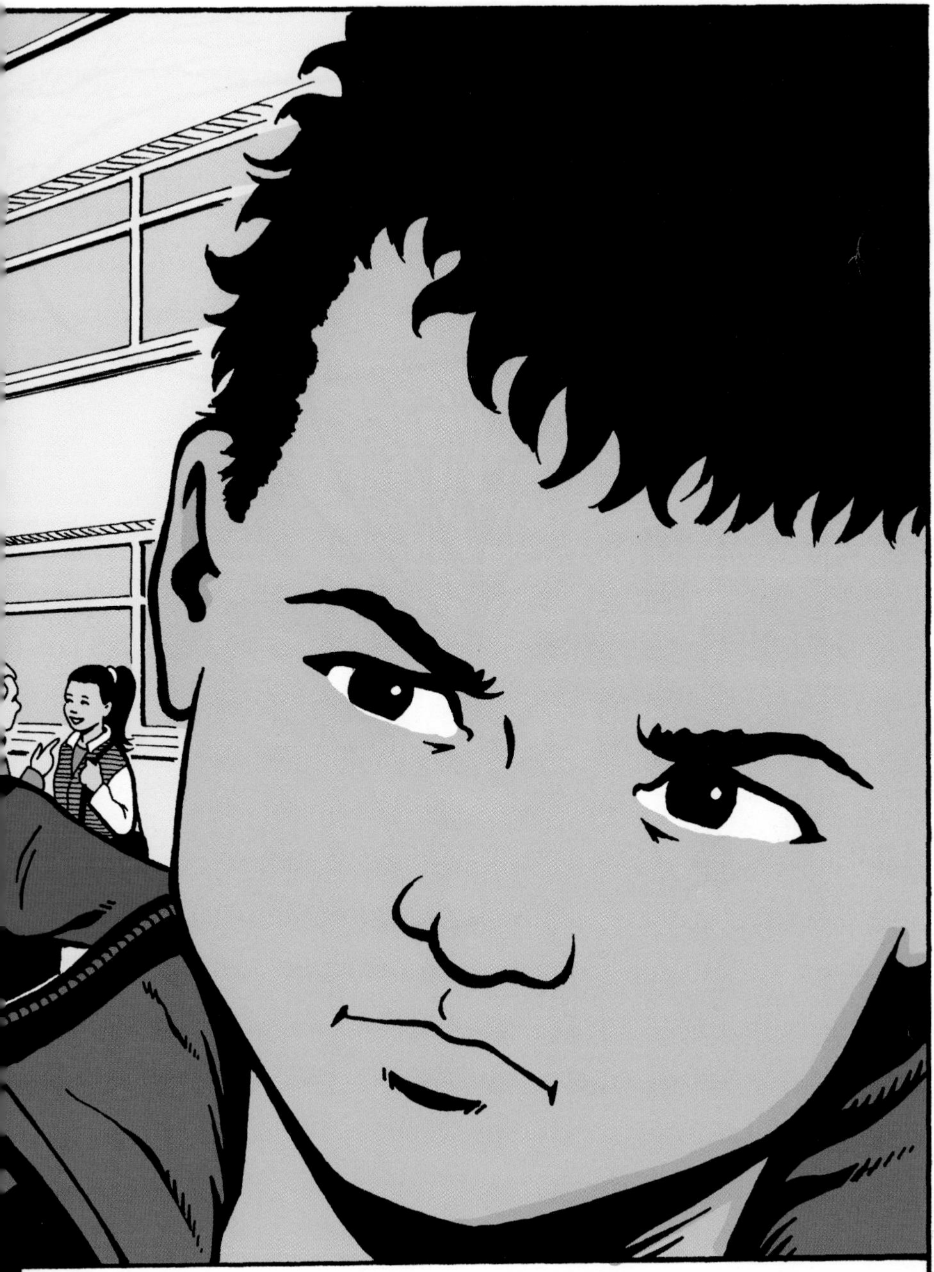

Sam couldn't prove it. He thought that at least Sallie would believe him, because she had seen him send the letter.

Chapter Five

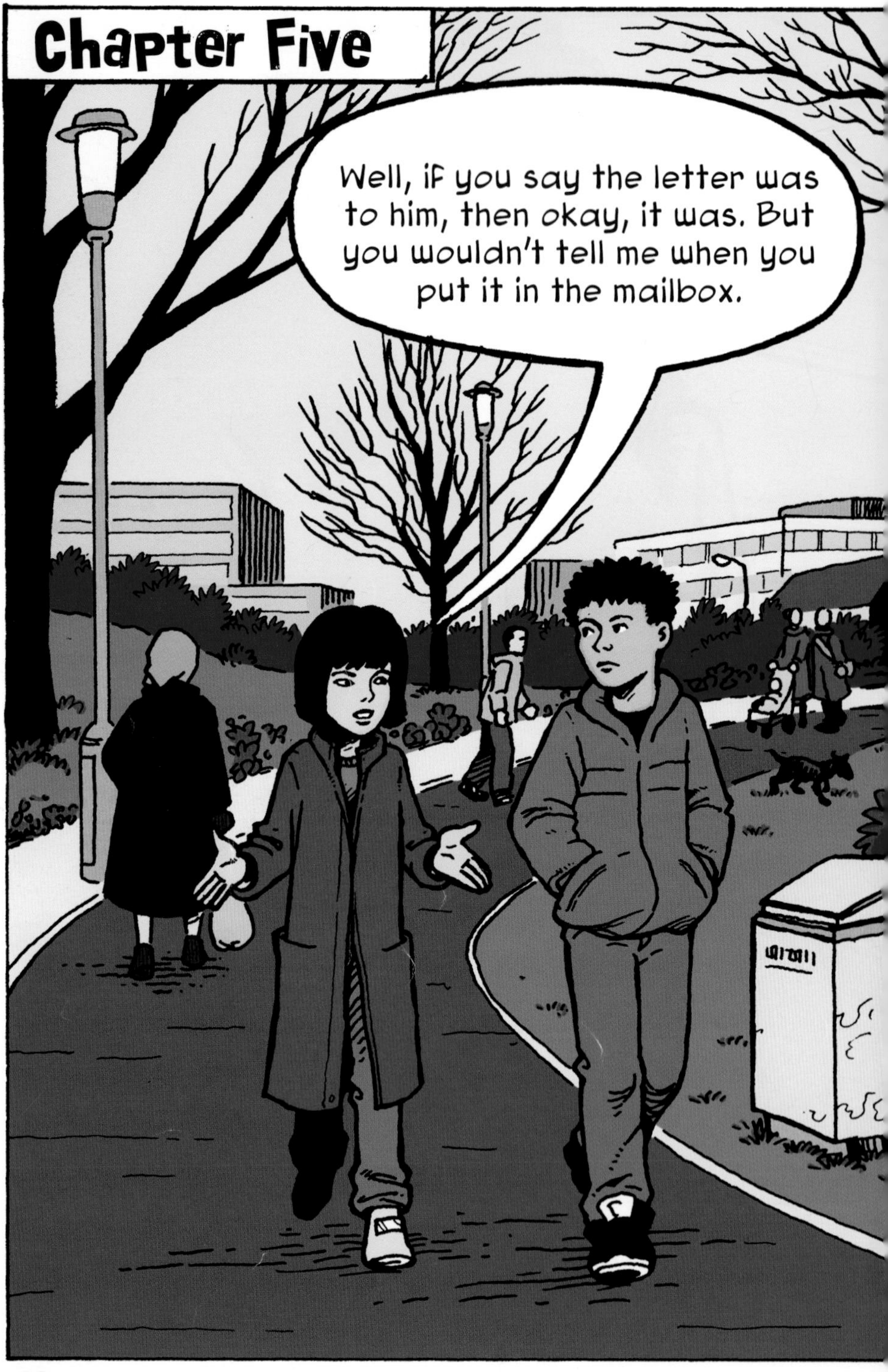
Well, if you say the letter was to him, then okay, it was. But you wouldn't tell me when you put it in the mailbox.

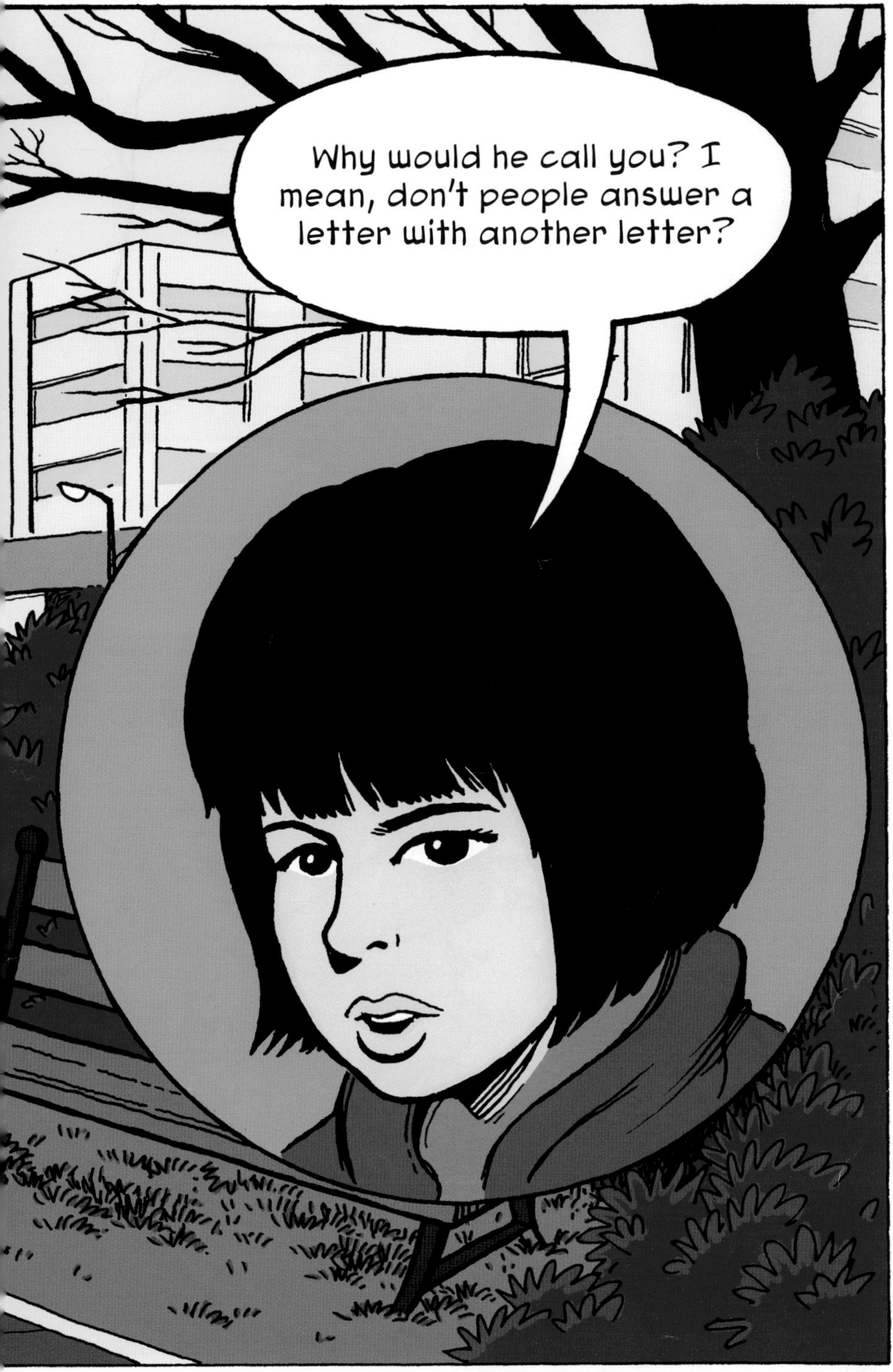
Why would he call you? I mean, don't people answer a letter with another letter?

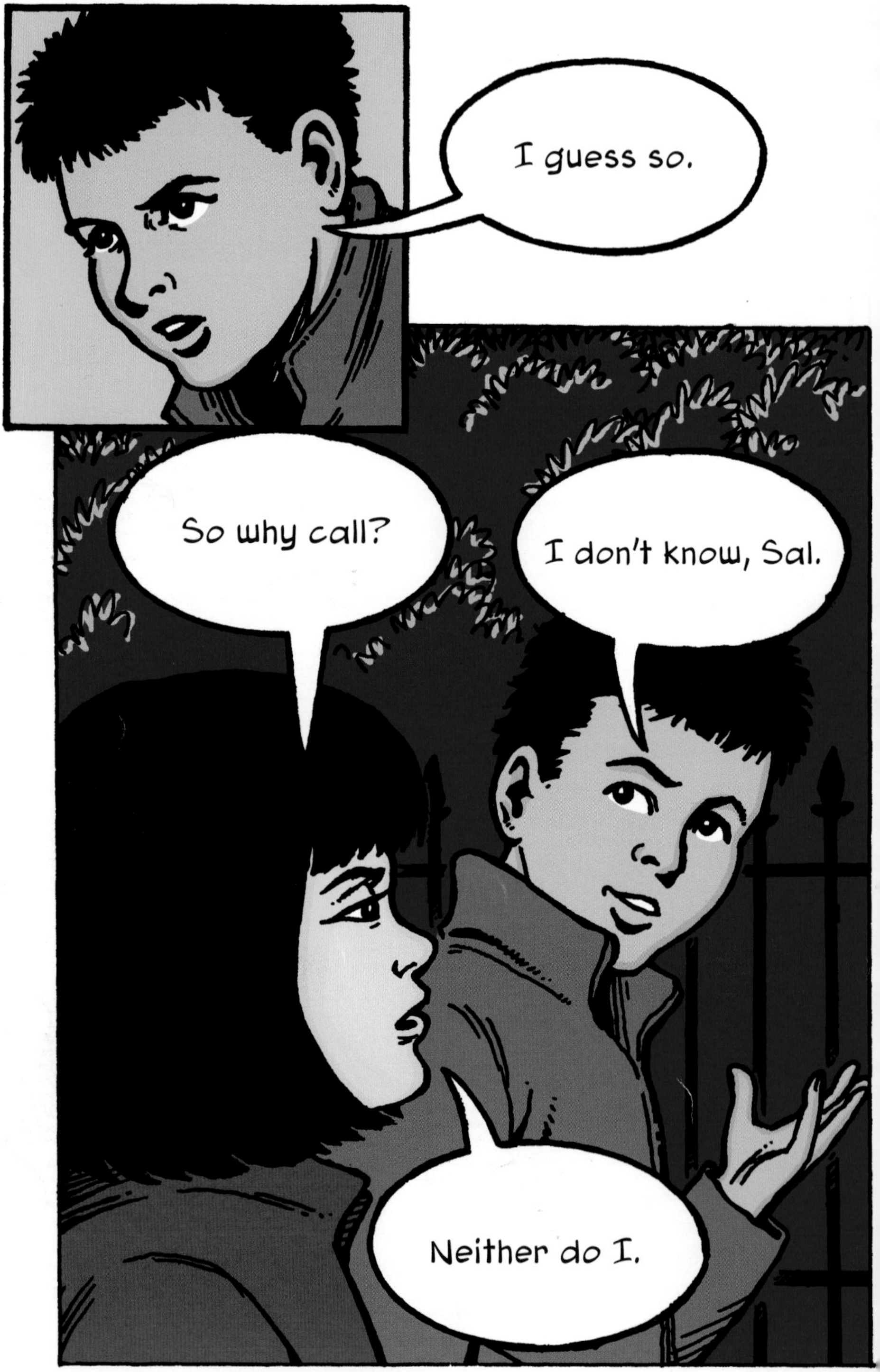
I guess so.
So why call?
I don't know, Sal.
Neither do I.

To try and prove he was in touch with the soccer star,
Sam trained harder than ever and practiced every night.

The coach was impressed.

You're making progress, Sam, no doubt about it. I'm sure your hero would want to sign you for the All Star Junior Team if he ever saw you in action!

But Sam didn't think his coach really meant that.

Then a card from Alex arrived in the mail on his birthday. It said "See you soon, Sam." But the signature was just a scrawl.

Once again, Sam's teammates didn't believe it was from the soccer star. It wasn't even signed "Alex Ackton." Sam wished he could call the All Stars player, but he didn't know his home number.

As the date of the Lightning's home game with the All Stars came closer and closer, Sam began to worry that Alex forgot his promise.

Sam couldn't stop worrying. On the day before the game, he felt so bad he didn't want to go to school. His dream had turned into a nightmare.

Yet, somehow, he got through the day. Antony had his own promise for him.

My mom says that if you don't get to go to the game, she'll take us somewhere special. She won't let us down, Sam.

Sam tried to smile.

I know.

Sam knew that if he didn't hear from Alex the next day, he'd want to hide away from everyone. He wouldn't be able to face anyone.

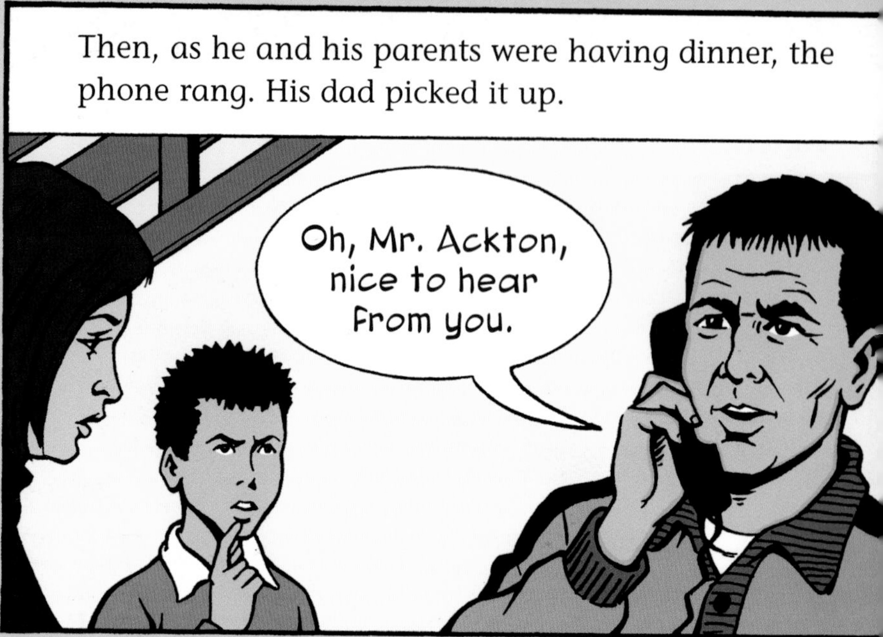
Then, as he and his parents were having dinner, the phone rang. His dad picked it up.
Oh, Mr. Ackton, nice to hear from you.

Sam jumped so high he thought he would hit the ceiling.

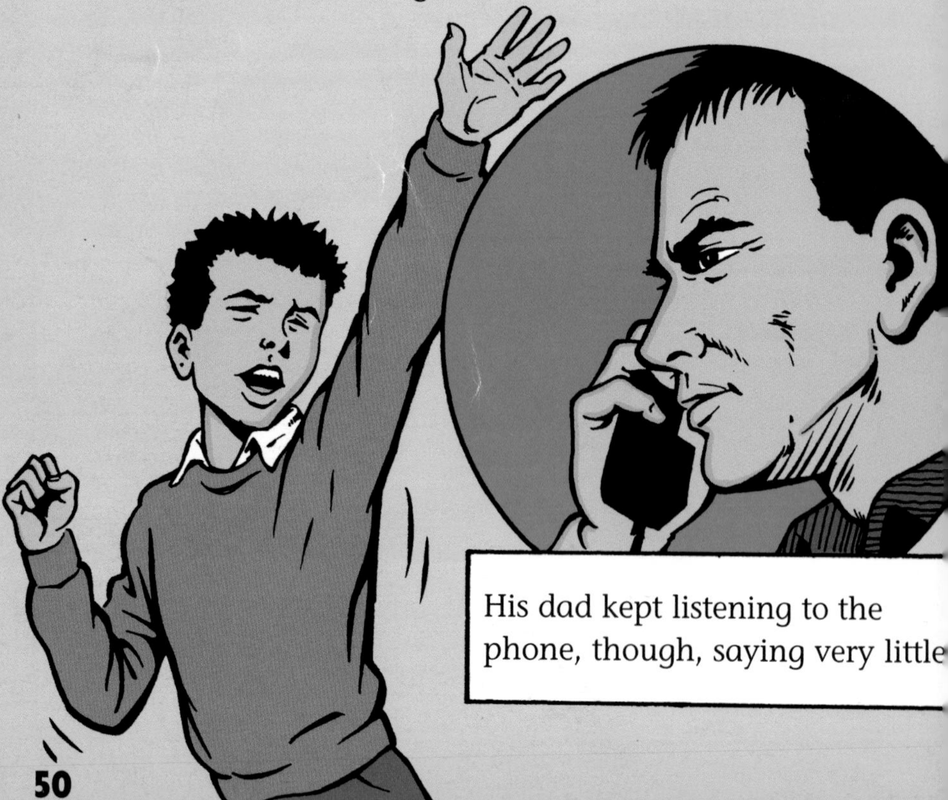
His dad kept listening to the phone, though, saying very little

Suddenly, Sam guessed the news was bad. Alex wasn't going to meet him after all.

Sam couldn't bear to listen. He even put his hands over his ears until he realized he couldn't hear what Alex was saying, anyway. Then his dad finished the phone call.

Sam's dad was smiling like a lottery winner.

Sam, you'll love this! Alex has arranged for you to be a ball boy for the All Stars tomorrow. So you'll get to go on the field with him before the game. He's even bringing you a team jersey to wear. I told him your size. When the game kicks off, you'll come and sit in the stands with your mom and me. Isn't that terrific?

Awesome!

Sam could hardly believe it. He was going to meet his hero tomorrow and walk onto the field with him.

Chapter Six

They got to the game early and went to the main office. Alex had arranged for them to be met by an official.

While his parents waited, Sam was taken to a locker room to change.

Someone gave Sam the ball boy
uniform, which he quickly put on.

Once he put on his soccer shoes, Sam was nervous. Was he ready for the greatest moment of his life?

They met as the players lined up in the tunnel leading to the field. Alex shook Sam's hand and ruffled his hair.

Great to meet you, Sam. Hope you're going to enjoy the game.

Sam didn't know what to say. He just beamed with excitement.

The crowd roared as the teams ran out into the sunshine. The noise was deafening. Sam had never played in front of so many people. It was almost scary.

Sam kept close to Alex during warm-ups. When Alex kicked a ball sideways to him, he knew what he was going to do.

He took the ball for a couple of paces and then fired it high into the top of the net. Alex clapped and called, "Good goal!" Sam was sure some of the cheering from the crowd was for him. It didn't matter if it wasn't, though. He had scored from a pass given to him by the world's best player.

Even the All Stars' goalkeeper gave him a thumbs-up as he grabbed the ball out of the net and kicked it to another player.

Things happened very quickly after that. The ref, the team captains, and the ball boys had their photos taken in the center circle. Sam was thinking that his Aces teammates would see him in the local paper with his hero. They'd see for themselves that he had been telling the truth.

The ref tossed a coin for choice of sides for kick-off. When the choice was made, he gave the coin to the Lightning's ball boy. Sam didn't mind. He had gotten something much more precious.

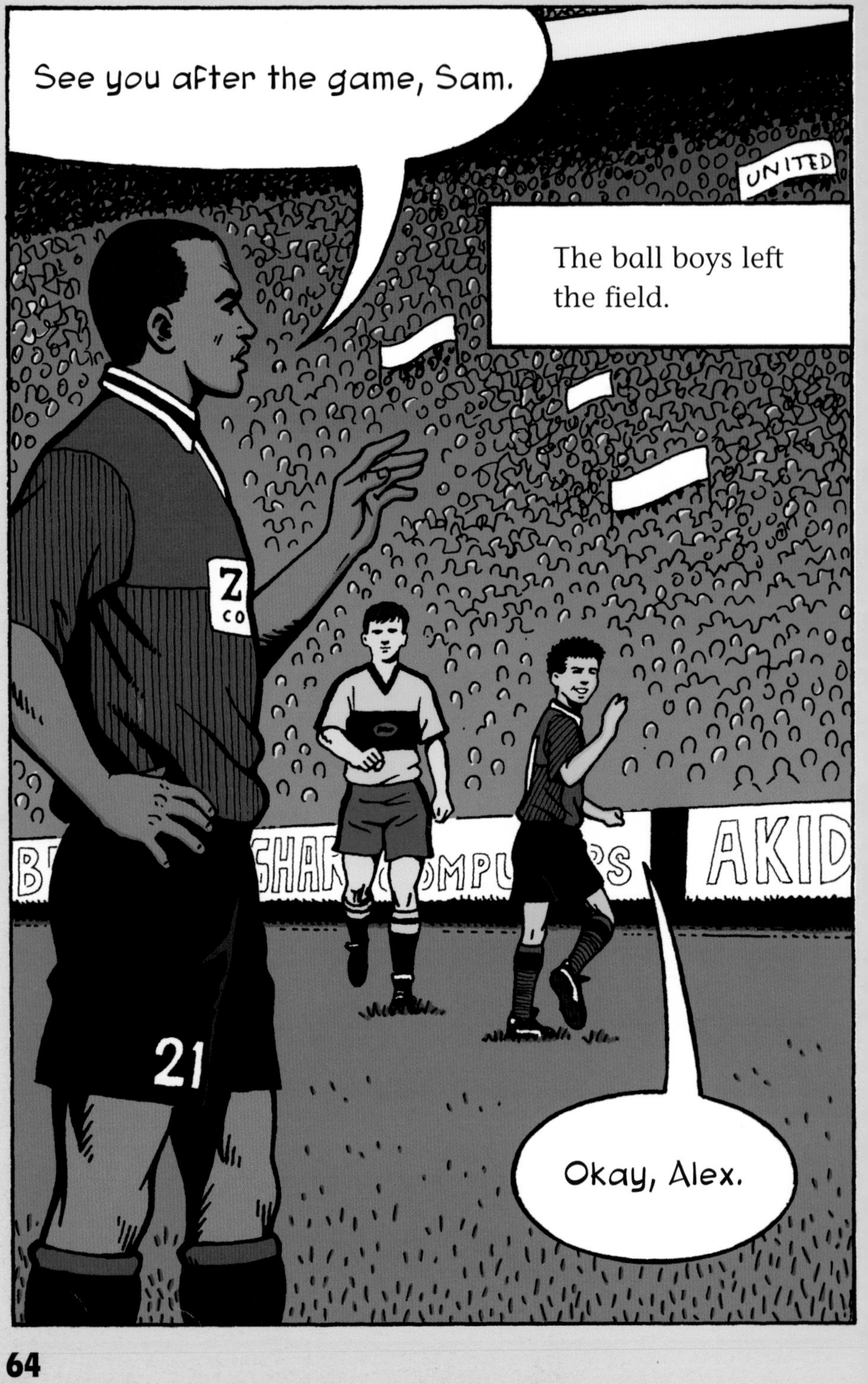
See you after the game, Sam.
The ball boys left the field.
Okay, Alex.
UNITED

Spectators grinned at him as he climbed the steps in the stands to sit next to his parents.

Sam paused and thought for a moment. Then he said happily:

ABOUT THE AUTHOR

Michael Hardcastle loves sports, and he spends his time writing about sports for children and young adults. He has written more than 90 books. He lives in Yorkshire, England, and loves talking to children about writing.

GLOSSARY

autograph (AW-toe-graf)—a person's handwritten name

contribution (kon-truh-BYOO-shun)—something you give or make for someone else

disappointed (dis-uh-POYNT-ud)—sad, upset

goal (GOHL)—meaning 1: something wanted and worked for

goal (GOHL)—meaning 2: an area on a soccer field into which a player must get a ball in order to score

profile (PRO-fyle)—a report on a famous person, usually written in a newspaper or magazine

stunned (STUHND)—overwhelmed; shocked

version (VURR-zhun)—a different form of something, such as a letter or written report. When you write a letter, you might write several different versions before you come up with one you like.

wail (WALE)—a cry or shout

INTERNET SITES

Do you want to know more about subjects related to this book? Or are you interested in learning about other topics? Then check out FactHound, a fun, easy way to find Internet sites.

Our investigative staff has already sniffed out great sites for you!

Here's how to use FactHound:

1. Visit *www.facthound.com*

2. Select your grade level.

3. To learn more about subjects related to this book, type in the book's ISBN number: **1598890883**.

4. Click the **Fetch It** button.

FactHound will fetch the best Internet sites for you.

DISCUSSION QUESTIONS

1. Look at the definitions (in the glossary) of "goal." Which meaning was the author thinking of when he chose the title of this story? Explain your thinking.

2. What do you think of the coach's responses to Sam on pages 8 and 9? How would you feel if a coach treated you that way? Explain.

3. If you had the chance, what (sports) celebrity would you invite to a party? Explain who you would ask and why.

4. Sallie was surprised that Alex called Sam but did not write back to the letter. Why do you think he called instead of writing back?

WRITING PROMPTS

1. Sam's letter got results! Write a letter to someone famous, inviting them to do something with you, or for you.

2. What dream do you have that you wish could come true? Write about it.

3. Pretend you are a famous person. What would you be famous for? If you received an invitation to a fan's party, would you go? Write what you would say back to your fan.

ALSO BY MICHAEL HARDCASTLE

My Brother's a Keeper

It looks like the Raiders are out of luck when their goalie gets injured before the big game. Luckily, Carlo, one of the team's top scorers, has a new stepbrother who just happens to play goal.

Archie's Amazing Game

Archie's mom has banned him from playing soccer. Can he use his sister and best friend to get back in the game without their knowledge?

STONE ARCH BOOKS,
151 Good Counsel Hill Drive, Mankato, MN 56001
1-800-421-7731
www.stonearchbooks.com